A Treasury of Short Stories

Neha Bansal

best wishes
from
Bansal

PUBLISH AMERICA

PublishAmerica
Baltimore

First printing

ISBN: 1-4137-6025-2
PUBLISHED BY PUBLISHAMERICA, LLLP
www.publishamerica.com
Baltimore

Printed in the United States of America

For my mother and father.

Contents

SAKI 7

Lost 23

The Painter 33

The Empress' Jade Necklace 41

Lucia 47

SAKI

About two hundred miles southeast from a small village in Nepal, Pokhara, there lay a great jungle, stretched across vast amounts of land, which was all ruled by Saki. To outsiders, he was known as the Great Shere Khan, but to the people of this village, he was Saki, which means "the great one." Every living creature upon the earth feared him immensely, and thus respected him. Saki was the only Caspian tiger left in the world.

He usually liked to go out at night and take a long stroll through his kingdom and enjoy the tranquil sounds of the waterfalls. All was silent at this time, except for the occasional chirps of a grasshopper, the cries of a lost panther, or the grunt of a wild boar, as he dug up his favourite root. However, the sounds eventually faded as the faint breeze carried them along into the distance.

Hunters from all across the world had tried to capture

Saki, each having failed horribly, and most having died a painful death. Back in northwest Virginia, an ex-military officer, now known as Leo, had always had a keen interest in tigers. He had decided that he wanted to set out on his own mission to track down Shere Khan. Before he became a military officer, he was a zoologist, and still he had a keen interest in studying animals, especially tigers.

Leo had had some past experience with tigers, because he also used to work in a zoo in Florida before going into the military service. He had worked with many animals there. Although he knew that going into a jungle full of wild animals was not quite the same, he still pursued the idea and took a flight to Nepal as soon as possible.

When he arrived at the airport in Kathmandu, he hired a driver for two days to take him to Pokhara. From Pokhara, the driver took him to the jungle, and fled as soon as he could from the site, because of knowing what lived there. Even the area around the jungle was deserted; there were no people living within fifty miles of the jungle.

Leo opened his eyes wide to the entrance of the jungle, which forebodingly emerged and proceeded forward. He walked for many hours, taking only a few minutes rest here and there. As nightfall approached, he decided to recline underneath a large palm tree. He kept a sharp knife close to him as he slept, just in case.

The rays of the sun shone powerfully, and the intense heat caused Leo to awake immediately. Finally it was morning, and he heaved a sigh of relief, as he had survived the first night. He got up and continued with his trek. On his way, he stopped for breakfast at a tall mango tree and packed a few more in his bag for later. The atmosphere seemed so peaceful and calming that for a moment he forgot all about the tiger.

He walked along the paths of the jungle, sometimes bobbing his head slightly to avoid the hanging foliage. He walked for many hours and then suddenly came to a halt when he began to hear a soothing sound. He peered through the bushes and caught sight of the most beautiful thing he had ever seen. It was a large waterfall behind a glowing rainbow. He stared at this magnificence for quite some time, until it was dark again. He was so amazed by this sight that he decided he would rest there until morning. There was a full moon that night and Leo lay there on the ground with a few soft leaves under his head, which served as a pillow, as he gazed up at the clear sky while listening to the singing of the waterfall to lull him asleep.

The next morning, he was awakened by a group of voices. It seemed to be getting closer and closer, and with an overwhelming event of anxiety and fear, he made for the bushes and hid. He tried to calm himself with the reassurance that the voices were at least human. He felt silly being so cowardly he was supposed to be here, searching for the fiercest tiger in the world and yet he was afraid of humans! But, as always, he let his imagination get the best of him, and began thinking of the wildest things.

What if they're cannibals? Or tribal people who want to take me away for a sacrifice, or …

At last, his curiosity was over when he saw their faces. It was the military soldiers; he knew every single one of them, as he used to work with them back home in Virginia, until the head military officer fired him and burned all records of his existence. They had accused him of giving out classified information about a particularly "important" (illegal) project. In actual fact, Leo had not disclosed any information about it—he didn't even understand it, but at the time all appearances were against him and he had no evidence to support his argument. The project was something about regenerating the dead cells of both humans and animals, in order to bring them back to life. They were digging up some of the graves of dead people from the local cemeteries and conducting some experiments. Whether they were successful or not didn't really present much of an interest to Leo.

As he lay low in the bushes, like a tiger, watching his prey before getting ready to pounce, he listened carefully.

"Agent Greene, you and your team cover the eastward section and keep your radios tuned in. Lie low, and the first sign of it, you call for backup immediately. Understood?"

"Yes, sir." The general then gave out the rest of his orders in a similar manner and finally asked, "Any questions?" The soldiers stood tall with their heavy gear, ready for action and said nothing.

"No? Good. Now go." The general spoke in a firm voice and kept a stern, alert expression on his face. The soldiers saluted him and headed out as instructed to, into their designated areas.

Leo suddenly realized that they were hunting Saki. They were after him; they wanted him for their project. The thought of it made Leo feel uneasy and fearful. He knew that if anyone had the power to hurt this tiger, it would be them. They had their expensive machinery, advanced locating systems, and various other gadgets, high technology weapons and not to mention strength and courage, which he had seen, proved many times to bring them success in their assignments. Looking at them, Leo felt very discouraged—with their skills and resources, he had no chance.

Nevertheless, he continued, but now with extra caution. If the soldiers found him, it would be the end for both his mission and most probably his life, too. He sustained with determination and acted on his instincts. In the past they had proven to be useful to him and had not yet let him down.

As he walked on farther, he turned his full attention to what was in the middle of his path—footprints: footprints that were so large and definitely like that of a tiger. Now he was on the trail and a sense of excitement came rushing across his face. He leaned against a tree on the side and slowly sank down to the floor to sit down. He planted his hands firmly in the ground over the small shrub-like plants, shut his eyes and gave a tired and relieved sigh.

After a few minutes, he got up and carried on walking through the jungle. It hadn't been long when he realized that his left hand was itching so much, and a tingling pain started to get more frequent. When he looked down at his hand, it was red and inflamed. Leo did not consider it to be anything more than a nettle sting, until he became rather light headed and instantly collapsed with a loud thud. Several hours later, Leo was still lying there in the same place, unconscious. All of a sudden, loud cries came out, and a group of strange people came running towards him. They were wearing feather-made skirts, had strange paintings and symbols on their bodies and spoke in an entirely different language. It was clearly obvious that they were tribal men. They picked up Leo and carried him back to their home.

While the two men were carrying him through the

village, they called out the name Tembu many times. They took Leo into a small hut, where they carefully laid him down on a straw mattress. They stood and watched him with the closest attention as they waited. Less than five minutes later, a middle-aged, dark, thin, bald man came running in with a little pouch attached to his waist. The man sat beside Leo and placed his hand on his forehead. He seemed to know exactly what was wrong, and in that instant, he called the other men to him and instructed them to go and get him some materials. Without any questions, they did as he asked. This man was a much respected member of this tribe, and he was known as Tembu, which means "the miracle worker."

Without any delay, they ran out as fast as they could, and quickly returned with a wooden bowl of water, a cloth, and a bundle of massive leaves. They were not like any regular leaves that you happen to pick up while having a stroll in your garden, truly they were huge. Tembu shoved his hand into his little pouch, looking for something, when at last he found it. It looked like a dried, cut open fig, but it was something much more extraordinary than that. No one was sure what it was, and no one ever dared to ask. They simply knew that whatever it was, it was powerful and they left it at that. Tembu held the fig-like object loosely in the palm of his hand, and extracted something seed-like from it, and placed it in Leo's mouth.

Following this, he began a sort of incantation and at once everyone else in the room fell silent. Meanwhile, the two men sat on the floor and each took a wide-surfaced, clay bowl. Then they grabbed two leaves and placed them inside their bowls, and each took a pestle-shaped object, which were actually elephant's tusks. With the elephant tusks, they both began to grind the leaves, and every so often they would mix a few drops of water until it became a thick paste. They went towards Leo, where Tembu was also sitting. Once more, Tembu gave his orders to the men and so they obeyed. They started to rub the paste all over Leo's body, and when they had finished, Tembu and the other men left.

Many hours later, Leo slowly opened his eyes. The surroundings were very blurred, and he could just see a hint of moonlight in the sky and a few twinkling stars around it. Gradually, the haziness started to clear up, and in alarm, Leo suddenly got up. He looked around the room, wondering where he was and trying to recall what had happened. Then he remembered that his hand was in pain and the last thing he felt was being dizzy. Thinking of this, he looked down at his hand and scrunched his face at the horrible sight of it. His whole body was covered in green, smelly paste.

Next, Tembu, the "doctor" (miracle worker), entered with a slight smile on his face. He walked towards Leo while he spoke, but Leo couldn't understand anything—he just sat there on the straw bed staring at Tembu's face. Then it seemed like he started to speak in another language completely, but still Leo could not answer.

Finally, after several language changes, Leo replied, "My name is Leo, but what am I doing here? Who are you?"

"I am Tembu. I belong to the Baldeo tribe. Some of our men were out hunting for food when they found you, lying on the floor, unconscious. They brought you here, and when I came to you, you were running a high fever. That must have been because of the beetle plant poison. We found that next to you; you must have touched it."

Leo noticed that although Tembu had a strong accent, his English was very good and also easy to understand. These people didn't seem like they wanted to sacrifice him, so he began to slowly trust them.

"Beetle plant poison?" he questioned.

"Yes, it is one of the most deadly poisons in the jungle. If you had been there for a few hours more in that condition, it would have been fatal," he added. "What are you doing here anyway?" he asked.

"I came here to look for the tiger, Saki. I did n—"

"You must leave, now. How dare you come here with your weapons to hunt the great Saki?" He spoke with great anger but at the same time with fear in his voice.

"No, no, I don't want to kill him ... I, eh ... came here to see what the world fears most and see whether it really is true that he exists. I can see that even by mentioning his name, you jumped!"

"You're mad, maybe I was wrong; the poison has made you insane! I have not cured you at all! You must leave this place. Return to your home, or else Saki will kill you. What did you think ... that he'll come to you and say, 'It's okay to take some photographs of me and I won't kill you'?" His sarcasm was rather amusing to Leo, and he struggled to keep his amusement hidden. He was scared that he might burst into laughter any moment!

"Well, you see, it's much more than that now. The military soldiers are after Saki, and they'll take him back to the main base in Virginia. There's a special lab there where the world's most renowned scientists work. They want to use him in their experiments and do all kind of horrible things to him." Leo's voice was almost in a pleading tone. "If they succeed in their experiments, we could all be in terrible danger."

"What kind of experiments?" Tembu looked at Leo with an eager and intrigued expression.

"Well, I'm not a hundred percent sure ... I mean they will be conducting many. But they will definitely use their probes and injections to modify his behaviour first."

"Why?" he asked.

"I just don't know," he replied.

"Well, what do you plan to do?"

Leo wasn't sure at all, but felt he should tell him something.

"I'll get there before the soldiers do and stop them," he said firmly.

"And ... you will do this all by yourself? Also, risk your own life to save a fierce tiger that has been known to kill hundreds of people? I'm sure he doesn't need your help. You really cannot make matters any worse, it would be best for you to just leave," Tembu advised him.

"You don't understand ... these soldiers have the weapons and power to kill this tiger," Leo assured.

"Why do *you* care so much?" Tembu questioned, with a sense of curiosity and surprise in his tone. Leo had nothing to say and simply shrugged his shoulders.

"Well, we can do nothing more than to accompany you in search of Saki. I will let the other men know that we are leaving at the break of dawn. You can wash up and take something to eat. You have not yet got your full strength back," he said, leaving the hut.

"Wait ... you're not coming with me!" Leo argued, running after him.

Tembu turned around, gave him a plain smile, and nodded his head once before he continued walking towards the other huts to inform the men about the plan. They gathered all of their essentials, which were mostly weapons, and some food.

At the break of dawn, they set off for their journey, as scheduled the day before. They walked for many miles until the sun began to set, and as they were so tired, they thought it best to rest for a few hours.

Night had only just given place to day the following morning when Tembu called everyone and urged them to wake up. He seemed to be rather agitated to make a start. They gathered all of their belongings together and set off once more in search of Saki. Leo complained of feeling rushed, as he didn't even have time to enjoy the interesting smells that the jungle holds in the morning.

They carried on with their journey, listening to the echoing sounds of various creatures and cautiously keeping their eyes focussed on the surroundings. Once or twice they would catch a glimpse of a mongoose or a gaur. They were not so alarmed by the gaur however, as they were comforted with the knowledge given from Tembu that the gaur only feeds on grass and shoots of bamboo and trees.

They encountered many meetings with jackals, foxes, and even a wild boar, but the tribal men were brave and fierce and were able to handle them all. Although their weapons were not quite as advanced as the soldiers', they still served their purpose perfectly.

Later the party reached a marsh, which indicated that crocodiles, snakes, and deadly fish were close by. Tembu quickly consulted Leo and told him what should be done in order to overcome this dangerous situation.

"I think I know a route that will take us around the

marsh, but it will take more time, and we still don't know how far the soldiers are. We must also hurry, though. It is said that crocodiles can smell their food from far away!"

Leo promptly confirmed, "Right, let's go."

It wasn't long until the men began to tire and felt in need of a break, so they found a small lantana bush nearby and decided to sit and relax for a while. The wonderful smells of the beautiful plants were so soothing and pleasant that the men could easily and comfortably unwind for a while.

Leo was leaning against a fig tree, when suddenly, one of the tribal men got up and casually threw a dagger towards him. It seemed too late for him to do anything when he caught sight of it, as it was flying through the air at such tremendous speed. He was about to scream, when he saw it fly past him and firmly plant itself in the tree. His heart was now racing ten times faster than the speed of a cheetah, when he saw the rock python attached to it, dangling down by the side of the tree. Leo looked up at the man who had thrown the dagger, and calmly shuffled his way far away from the tree, towards the bushes. He felt his stomach twist and turn in such a way that he had never felt before, and a look of pure disgust and discomfort came upon his face that he couldn't control. The group of men sitting next to the lantana bush burst into laughter, which was so uncontrollable that they were on their backs, rolling around in the foliage, clutching their stomachs in pain of laughter. Leo finally came out from the bushes and sat down beside them; their laughter suddenly stopped and they stared at his face. An uneasy smile crept across his face and at once they were off again in hilarity!

Since it was getting dark now, they decided to sleep for a few hours and make an early start the next day.

It was just before dawn, and everyone was awake and ready to go. Walking along their way, a leopard joined the scene. The leopard stayed low and was as quiet as a mouse. No one saw it until it stepped clear of the thick undergrowth, came to a stand, and then looked back over his shoulder. He was a large creature with fiery eyes. He had a beautiful, glossy coat, and the rosettes on his skin stood out like clear-cut designs on a rich, velvet material. At once the men took out their weapons and immediately focussed all of their attention onto the leopard.

They were trapped and knew that they couldn't escape because the leopard would easily outrun them, and one of them would pay a heavy price. Labhu, who was one of the tribal men, was a very cunning and brave man. With all his courage, he ran past the leopard as fast as he could, but the leopard was quicker, and the others only just managed to see his hind quarters and tail disappear behind the bushes. They were all fearful for Labhu, and when they heard the outcries of pain coming from the bushes, they immediately rushed to his aid. One of the men crept up behind the leopard, and with a large knife, stabbed the leopard repeatedly until it backed away, limping, leaving a small trail of blood. The leopard collapsed and lay there in the bushes, still. It was probably dead, or dying. However, they could not be sure, so they thought it best to end the leopard's misery quickly. While everyone's attention was diverted towards Labhu, Leo took care of the deed.

Labhu was severely injured, as half of his leg had been chewed off, and he had suffered some injuries to his head and face. Tembu came running and attended to him. The others were in a state of shock and horror at the sight, and they were filled with sadness. Tembu reassured them that he would soon recover, but it was certain that he would be handicapped. One person volunteered to stay behind and look after Labhu until he felt well enough to make their way back home. The others, feeling distraught, knew that they must go on in order to complete this mission.

The next morning, they were very close now. Saki could be anywhere in this area, but also the soldiers could be near, too. They kept extra caution and every so often they jolted their heads back or to the side quickly, diligently scanning the bushes and always listening closely for the slightest sniff or growl. Every step they took was always with great vigilance. It wasn't a long time that they had been walking when a group of grey clouds gathered together in the sky, blocking the sun, and in that instance, everything became dark and dull. An expression of terror arrived on Tembu's face, as he quietly spoke, "This is a bad omen."

Suddenly an extremely violent, cyclonic storm struck in this part of the forest. The storm caused a series of horrific events, uprooting a number of trees, causing them to tumble with a mighty crash, resulting in an earthquake-like tremor. Animals rushed here and there, and the small ones scurried away as fast as they could towards shelter. Panic struck the entire forest, and at this point, every animal and human was feeling the same thing—terror.

The rain hit hard and heavy like it did in the monsoon season. The marshes quickly flooded and the crocodiles quickly gathered their young and made their way out of the marshes. Leo watched with fear and amazement from underneath the shelter of the collapsed trees as all the animals dealt with this event. The animals were close to their young, watching over them and making sure that they were away from any danger.

As he stood there, he noticed a small tiger cub all on his own, next to a hibiscus bush. The cub was so cute and innocent, with his coat covered with orange and black irregular stripes. He waited a while to see if a relation to the cub came to his rescue, but no one came. Without further hesitation, he ran to the cub, scooped him up in his arms, and carried him back to the safe spot underneath the wreck of the trees. The cub snuggled up into his arms, feeling a sense of security.

Gradually, the storm started to calm down, and consequently so did the animals. Leo put the cub down and urged him to run along. The cub took no notice and made up his mind to follow him. He smiled at the cub and finally agreed to this arrangement.

Some time later, they stopped for a drink at a waterfall when they caught sight of him. It was Saki—standing tall with all his might, and even his presence gave out strong vibes of extreme power and authority. He roared and all the sounds of the jungle stopped at once. It became a deathly silence, as even the crickets and grasshoppers stopped chirping. Everything was still. Saki looked at Leo, who was holding the cub.

The tiger began to walk towards him and then came to a halt, letting out a loud, painful cry. Saki had been hit with a tranquillizer, but this was not enough to bring him down. The tribal men caught sight of the soldiers running towards them, firing many times at Saki, yet he maintained his strength. An ugly war broke out between the tribal men and the military men, and the soggy, black soil gained a reddish tint from all the bloodshed.

While fighting, Leo glanced across at Saki, and realised something extraordinary. Saki had a distinct dark feature above his left eye. It was a large, black blob, and the cub that he had found also had exactly the same feature in exactly the same place. *How is this even possible? This would mean that Saki is not the only Caspian tiger in existence!*

Saki's health was deteriorating fast, and the situation did not look promising. The fighting between the men was almost over, as many deaths had occurred on both sides, and many of the soldiers began to surrender. All was coming to a standstill when at once, one of the soldiers charged at Saki with a long sword, and everyone paused with a look of horror upon their faces as they watched Saki sink into the ground. The soldier grinned and turned his back, but Saki was not going to let him go that easily. He pounced on him from behind and instantly killed him. The remaining soldiers escaped by showing a clean pair of heels.

Saki collapsed on the ground and let out a huge, heroic, final roar. He looked at the cub sitting beside him in a soft, caring way, and there he took his last breath.

Leo looked at the tiny cub and he was sure that he was the son of Saki. He did not tell any of the tribal men about this, though, and assumed that they had not noticed, which was true for all of them except one.

He didn't have the heart to leave the cub alone in the forest; so together they took a step forward, embarking on a new life together.

Lost

I could not remember how long I had been travelling and I had no idea where I was. All I could fathom was that I was in a desert. It was hot and sandy. I knew that the desert was screaming with wildlife, but the atmosphere seemed almost silent to me. All I could hear were the chirrups of a dragon fly, and the shrill cry of a cicada.

The sandy desert floor had wavy patterns imprinted into it, where snakes had slithered their way across it. These minute grains of sand cushioned themselves irritably between the toes of my feet, the sweltering heat made my cheeks blush, and salty droplets of water trickled down the sides of my face. Time was of no meaning to me now, and I had lost track of how many days I had been here. The beauty of the desert amazed me, and every so often, a gentle breeze would swing by and glaze my face with a second of coolness. My jeans were torn and my white shirt was stained and my open flat sandals were not able to refuse the incoming tides of the silky sand.

There were a few cacti that I used to quench my thirst. It took me at least half an hour to cut through the fleshy, meaty stem of the cactus with my Swiss-Army knife, while avoiding the stinging spikes. It was quite a skilful task, which I grew better at as time went on. The cactus was satisfying and refreshing. At night I decided to make a small fire nearby with twigs and leaves that I had gathered. I took some cactus and roasted it on the fire. This had been a staple diet of mine ever since I landed here in the desert: roasted cactus on the side of a baked lizard, or any other animal that I could find and catch.

Despite my longing to return home, I began to enjoy and appreciate the ways of the desert. In the daytime the intense heat of the sun filled the air and the pale blue azure was calm. The sun penetrated my skin and made me feel uncomfortably sticky and hot. At night, the beautiful blue-black velvet sky was cool, and the moon and stars glistened brightly, as powerful as the sun itself.

While I was wandering through the desert, nightfall was approaching, so I decided to rest and find a cosy spot where I could sleep. I found a comfortable place behind a large rock.

I woke up the next morning when the bright rays of the sunlight touched my face. I immediately glimpsed three figures slowly moving towards me. As they approached nearer and nearer, the three strange figures began to transform into a rather large, round man, a short, rounded woman, and an Arabian camel.

The man and woman were both dressed in black, which seemed extremely absurd, due to the extreme heat of the desert. The man was dressed in a black cotton *abaya* and had a grey-black, long beard. He also wore a black, embroidered *taqiah* on his head. The woman was dressed in a black *gambaz,* which covered her right down to her ankles. She also wore a black *mandeal* and so the only thing that could be seen were her piercing, blue-grey eyes. The camel that was trailing behind them was loaded with what seemed like bundles of clothes and fabrics.

They approached me and introduced themselves. Then the man asked me who I was and what I was doing out here all alone in the desert.

"Hello. I am Abdul and this is my wife, Yasmin."

"Hey, my name's David. I'm a pilot. I was flying my plane out here, and the engine failed. My plane crashed somewhere back there ..." I said pointing my finger out into the opposite direction from where we were standing.

"Oh, my goodness! Was there anyone else with you?"

"Yes, a friend, but when I regained consciousness after the crash, I found him lying next to me, dead."

"Oh, I'm so sorry for your loss."

"Thank you." I decided to swiftly change this morbid topic of conversation and asked him, "So, what are you doing out here?"

"My wife and I are in the trading market. We grow lots of different types of tea back home in Egypt. We are now on our way to Libya to sell and trade our goods."

"So what kind of tea are you transporting now?"

"Oh this?" Abdul pointed to the large bundles strapped to the camel. "This is mainly hibiscus tea leaves, and here, in this box are some of our finest pieces. Here, I'll show you."

Abdul signalled to his wife and told her to take out a piece from the box. She brought it to him, and he wiped of the tiny dust particles using the bottom of his black cloak. He then carefully handed it to me. This tiny teacup was magnificent and fragile. It was pink stained glass, with intricate gold patterns all over it, and it had pink sapphire stones lining the edges.

"This is exquisite. It must be very expensive!" I queried.

"Yes, each piece is worth 300 Egyptian pounds."

The box was filled with similar handmade teacups, and each cup was unique and had different designs on it. The colours had a wide range, from pearl white, to lilac amethyst.

I decided to accompany them for a while on their journey through the desert. A few hours later, we came to a tent that belonged to Abdul. He said he made these journeys through the desert very often, so he set up his own tent here where they could stop over and rest at nighttime. Abdul and Yasmin seemed to be nice people, although Yasmin never made any eye contact or spoke a word to me throughout the whole journey. Abdul was quite a flamboyant character with a good sense of humour. He was very talkative and it was evident that he had had a lot of different kinds of experiences in his life, and I felt that he was on a mission to tell me every single one of them before nightfall.

When reaching the tent, I was offered hospitality, and I was invited to share a small meal with Abdul and Yasmin. It suddenly occurred to me that neither of them had once stopped during their journey in the daytime to have something to eat or drink.

"You must be very hungry and thirsty, Abdul. You and your wife have not had anything to eat or drink all day!" I exclaimed.

"No, not at all. We do not have this craving or hunger for food and water while we are in the desert," Abdul replied.

"But how is this possible? That would be quite inhuman, don't you think?"

Abdul laughed and then spoke, "No, it's true! You see, before we set off on our journey, each morning we both drink this. Here, have some. It's very good!"

Abdul handed me a small teacup, which contained a very thick, warm liquid in it. I was a little cautious about drinking it, but I took a small sip anyway. I swallowed it with great difficulty, exclaiming, "What is that? Oh my goodness, that's awfully sweet. It's horrible!"

He laughed and then replied, "I'll tell you ... it's simply made from sugar and warm water."

"So that's it? That's all you have for the whole day ... Every day?"

"Yes, but only when we are in the desert, going on very long journeys like this."

"So that's why most of your teeth are rotting away then, Abdul?" I said jokingly.

Abdul began to laugh loudly and we were both in a laughing fit for the entire night.

Morning came and it was time for me to go my separate way. As I walked farther and farther, it seemed as though there was no end to the desert, and it seemed as though there was no civilisation for miles and miles. I grew tired of this nothingness. The silence and isolated feeling was maddening, and in a fit of extreme despair, I threw myself to the ground and lay there with the side of my face embedded in the sand. I lay there staring out towards the horizon for quite some time.

Suddenly I felt something crawling up my right

shoulder and I carefully turned my head to look over my shoulder. It was the first time I had ever seen a scorpion in real life—I had seen them before in movies, but seeing it so close was very frightening. Droplets of sweat began to pour down the sides of my face while I thought about how I should go about this. I brought my trembling, clammy left hand towards my right shoulder and quickly brushed away the scorpion. In an instant I was up on my feet, quickly running away from the site.

The next two days were long and hard, but on the third day, I came across a little girl, no more than the age of eight or nine. She seemed a little scared, so I did not attempt to introduce myself. When she ran away, I decided to follow her, since I thought I would be able to meet some other people and ask for help. I came to a stop when I reached an area of land where there were about 15 people. It was almost like a small tribe. Suddenly, one of the men caught sight of me and casually walked towards me, as though he knew me. Then he asked, "Who are you? What are you doing here? Were you stranded here or something?"

"No, my name is Ian, and I need to get home."

"Where are you coming from? If you need to get home, why are you wandering about in the desert?"

"I'm travelling from Egypt. I was on holiday there with my wife. A couple of weeks ago, she was murdered, and the police think that I did it. They took my passport so I couldn't leave the country, and they sent their officers after me. The only thing I could think of was to run, or else they would have thrown me in prison for a crime I didn't commit."

"So you didn't kill your wife?" the old man asked.

"No, of course I didn't!" I replied, irritated.

"Why are you running away then?" he asked patronizingly.

"They don't believe me, and the evidence that they claim to have found apparently proves that I'm the murderer."

"Where are you trying to get to now?"

"Well, I want to get to Chad, where my friend, Mekhiz, lives. I'll get a new passport made there and I'll get a flight back home to Boston."

Whether he believed me or not, that was my story, and after explaining the whole situation, I decided to appeal to him for help.

"Can you tell me where we are—what is this place called?"

"Certainly, this is the Sahara desert. You are at present in Sudan."

"This is the country, Sudan?"

"Yes. To get to Chad, you must go in that direction I think," he said, pointing his finger towards west.

I set off, on my way once again, but it was during this part of my journey that I encountered some disturbing events. As I walked farther, the desert began to change—it was not like it had been before and I no longer felt secluded.

I again came to a small holding, but there was no one there and everything had been wrecked. The tents were torn and turned upside down; there was no sound of any voices. The only thing that could be heard was the clattering of a few pots and pans. *Where could these people be?* I walked closer towards the ruins, and I began to hear a strange noise—I thought it was human, and so I slowly walked towards where it was coming from, and it led me to a small, ruined tent. I pulled away the cloth in front of it, only to find an elderly woman sitting there, with a red shawl wrapped around her. She was crying.

"What is the matter?" I asked. But there was no reply for a few minutes. I stood there, looking all around the tent, when suddenly she spoke. However, I could not understand what she was saying—she could not speak English. Then she got up and hobbled across the tent and from a wooden chest; she took out a small metal box. She came back towards me and sat down at the table, signalling me to do so, too, and I obeyed her instructions. I watched her closely as she opened the box, and she took out a pack of cards, it seemed. *This is not the time to be playing poker,* but I soon realised that these were not playing cards—they were tarot cards, so I concluded that she must be some sort of fortune teller.

She began laying down these cards with various pictures and I realised she was trying to tell me something. The first card had a picture of a woman holding a baby, the second had a picture of a dagger and blood, and the third was a picture of a wolf and the moon. She sat there in front of me, watching me, eagerly waiting for me to try and work out what she was trying to tell me, when suddenly I realised what had happened. *The people living here have been killed and she is upset because it was her family ... well, it is something like that.*

I looked at her and she knew that I understood. However, a few moments later, a look of terror crept up across her face, and she became so fearful that she immediately got up and backed away from the table. I turned around to see whether there was something behind me that was terrifying her so much, but I saw nothing. When I turned back round again, she appeared to be so scared. She attempted to scream, but when doing so no sound came out of her mouth and she instantly fell to the floor. I ran to her to check her pulse and found that she was dead.

I decided not to stay in this place any longer. I looked to see if there was any food or drink left here in the tent, and whatever I could find; I took with me and continued my journey. I did not attempt to look in the other tents as I thought that they may be covered in blood stains of the dead bodies. I did not exactly know what happened here, but this place reeked of death and I wanted to leave it as soon as possible.

After walking a few more miles, I came to a road and I sat on the side waiting for a car to pass by that would be willing to give me a lift. I waited for many hours until a black jeep drove up and I stretched out my hand, asking for a lift. They were a young couple and they seemed like nice people because they stopped and offered to give me a lift. Although, I could sense that the woman sitting in front of me felt a little uneasy and she did not seem too keen on the idea of inviting a stranger into her car.

"Hi, I'm Dan Isles, thanks a lot for giving me a lift—I really appreciate it."

"No problem. I'm Lucas and this is my wife, Anna. Do you live here in Chad?" the man asked.

"No, I'm only here because I'm an archaeologist and I believe that there is a site here in Chad that was home to a specific species of extinct tigers," I explained.

"Wow, that's quite interesting. What kind of tiger are you looking for then?"

"I'm sorry, I cannot share that piece of information with you."

"Okay, well where are you from, Dan?"

"I'm from Mexico—that's where I live," I replied.

As he turned around the bend, Lucas asked, "Is there any specific place where I can drop you off?"

"Well, may I ask where you are heading to yourself?" I inquired.

"We are going to the Ahaggar Mountains," he answered.

"They're in the Sahara Desert, aren't they?"

"Yes," he said. "You're welcome to join us if you like. You might find the bones and rocks that you're looking for there."

"All right then," I decided, spontaneously.

"What! No, he's not coming with us, Lucas, that's it! I want him to get out now—stop the car," Anna protested. At that moment, the woman turned around to face me, but she seemed disturbed and horrified. She just looked straight through me, as though I was not there. Then she started to scream loudly and she began to shout,

"Where is he? Where did he go?"

Her husband tried to calm her while apologising to me for her strange behaviour. He tried to make her understand that I was still in the car, sitting behind her. However, that just agitated her even more, and the situation soon began to get out of control. It was then that I decided to take action by thanking Lucas for the ride and telling him that I thought it best that I should leave and go my separate way. I got out of the car and looked up at the beautiful pink and red sky, and I wandered off towards the setting sun.

The Painter

Year 1891: Ruskin Berry

It was a dark, dreary night, and as the moonlight delicately touched the frosted and deserted surroundings, the town of Ruskin Berry lay in a deathly silence. It was occasionally broken by the shrill cry of a cicada, and the sudden crackle of the whirling leaves. There were only a few lanterns in the cobbled street that were lit.

The small, dark cottages on either side of the street led up to a rather small manor. There was a huge garden, in which several bushes were carefully positioned. These bushes had been made into models of horses, and there were also sculptures of abstract shapes that had been made from a metal-like substance.

The manor itself was quite intimidating, and had two cylindrical pillars at either side of the door. Through the tall, wooden, double doors, there was a narrow hallway, which was elaborately decorated. There was a series of paintings that hung on the walls, and a crystal chandelier that swayed from side to side even when the gentlest breeze touched it. After taking an immediate right turn into a large room, the first thing to catch the eye were the rich designs and colours on the walls. There were also blue velvet curtains with intricate, golden patterns, and heavy tassels swinging from them.

In the corner of the room, a thin figure sat perched on a high stool. His name was Edward Irving. In front of him, an easel stood with a canvas fixed to it. In his left hand, he held a pallet, and in his right, a fine brush with the wet bristles soaked in green paint. Beside him, he kept all his different sized brushes, acrylic paints, a pot of water, a small rag, and a little can of oil. The oil was used for his easel, as at times, while assembling it, the rusted, worn-out metal became stiff.

Edward loved to paint and had been doing it ever since the age of about five years. However, he had been shunned away by the townspeople because they thought that he was very peculiar and had no talent. Admittedly, his paintings were extraordinary, but this was what fascinated him. Though, gradually, after being discouraged and tormented by the people, he began to build hatred against them. Eventually, the warm-hearted and caring man had left from within him, and now all that was left was a bitter, lonely man.

One night while sitting in front of the fireplace, painting a new landscape, a young, mischievous boy could be heard running wild through the streets. He stopped in front of the large manor and approached it with a large rock in his hand. He waited a moment to make sure no one had caught sight of him, and then with all his might, he thrust it towards the window. The rock shattered the glass and hit Edward on the head, knocking him unconscious. As Edward fell to the floor, he also hit the oil can, causing it to spill. The oil caught on fire and the whole house burst into flames. As the flames raged in the manor, the townspeople watched, and yet no one came to his rescue. Edward Irving died, along with many of his paintings, which crumbled to ashes. However, one painting was left unharmed as it was kept in a special place, inside a glass case.

Present Day—2003: Ruskin Berry

The old, bare trees stood lifeless in the spiteful coldness of the town. Through the thick, grey mist, a black jeep drove up the street and parked itself outside an old derelict house. The whole town was in a haunting, quiet state. A young girl and her father stepped out of the car.

"What a beauty! Look, Zara! We'll make a few changes, and it'll be perfect!"

Zara stood still, wondering whether her father had gone insane. The house was in complete ruins, and she could not see the "beauty" in it at all. Another thing that she noticed was the fact that the townspeople were very odd, and they had no sense of fashion. Zara and her father decided to stay in a nearby apartment that they had rented for a few months until her father had finished renovating the house.

About three months later, they moved into their new house. To her great surprise, Zara found the house was amazing, and her excitement overpowered her as she ran through the doors to explore her home. She strolled around the house, inspecting each and every thing.

There was only one room left to see—the basement. She knew that the basement had not been fully renovated; however, her curiousness led her straight to the door. The cobwebs dangled from the low ceiling and stuck to her jacket as she pushed her way through. Shoved against the wall was a large glass case covered with a shroud-like shawl. When Zara pulled away the shawl, she found that it was a painting. It looked like the town that she was living in. The same trees, positioning of houses, cobbled streets with small houses lined against them. This painting fascinated Zara, as she too loved to paint. She decided immediately that she would try to make a copy of it. She got to work instantly, with the painting from the basement balanced beside her as a guide.

However, not long after she had started her painting, she knocked the pot of water onto the painting. As she got up to clean the mess, suddenly the table began to shake, the ornaments began to slide forward, and a sparkly, luminous light appeared in the middle of the painting. The light continued to grow larger and larger, until a tornado-like force hauled her into the painting.

A few moments later, Zara found herself in a strange but oddly familiar place. One thing she noticed straight away was that the people here behaved in almost the manner as where she lived. She looked around, puzzled, and rather afraid of what may happen next. A wooden post with the sign "Ruskin Berry" stood behind her, but when she saw it, she knew that this was not the town where she lived.

As Zara stood motionless and still confused, suddenly a tall shadow drowned her. She turned around quickly to see who it was, and found a stern-looking face staring down at her. He had a distinguished feature on his face that she noticed immediately. It was a small scar on the left side of his chin. He had short, curly, brown hair, a rather bulbous nose, beady eyes, and wore a long, black woolen coat.

"Who are you?" Zara questioned.

"I am Edward Irving, but who are you? I don't think I have ever seen you here before ... what are you doing here?" he asked.

She paused for a moment, Edward Irving? She felt that the name was familiar to her ... suddenly it clicked. She remembered the painting she had found in the basement and the small signature at the bottom of the canvas ... *Yes, it was made by him.*

"I'm Zara, and I came here through y ..." She hesitated as she thought that he probably would not believe her if she told him that she came through his painting, into this place—it was a bizarre thing to say, and hear.

"Yes, yes, carry on," he urged. Reluctantly she told him the truth and surprisingly, he didn't think of it as being strange at all.

Edward and Zara began to walk through the cobbled streets as they talked. First Zara told him everything about what had happened to her and about how she came about the painting. He then explained his history to her, and what happened with this town. He told her that everything that was happening in this world was the same as what was happening in her world, like a parallel world. It was as though he had cast a spell on the whole town, and made the townspeople suffer each day by being pulled into an everlasting silence and having to live in the past.

After listening to the full story, Zara became entangled in

a web of thoughts. Then she began waving her hands here and there as she spoke, "I understand that you are hurt. Nevertheless, taking eternal revenge on these people is not the way to go." Edward looked at her in an expression as if to say that she was a silly child who had no idea what she was talking about.

Standing firmly, he replied, "This is the only way, which will at least make me feel at peace."

"If you were at true peace, you wouldn't be stuck in this parallel world. You would be in heaven and your soul at rest … or something like that," she argued. "These people have suffered long enough, now stop this nonsense," she continued.

Taking a deep sigh, Edward stated that, "Even if I could, I wouldn't."

Getting frustrated by Edward's stubbornness, in anger she shouted, "Well fine then, at least send me back …" Before she could complete her sentence, she had disappeared and was now standing exactly in the same place as before in her house. The painting looked at her, but now in a way that she hadn't seen before. She felt that she had to do something to try and put things right. She did not know how she could help, and her anger overpowered her, making her come to the conclusion that she had to destroy the painting.

She set to work, trying to use different methods of destruction. The first thing that came to her mind was fire. Yet, when she bought the lighter within one centimetre of the painting, the flame blew out—this was no ordinary canvas painting. She also tried beating it with various objects that she could find, for example, a cricket bat, but it had no effect on the painting. She tried many times, and each time every method failed. Just as she was about to give up, something extraordinary happened.

A round, glowing orb appeared and lightly hovered above her. It was a large, bright, white light. It was some sort of mystical ball of energy that slowly began to move closer towards the painting. Zara cautiously stepped back, not knowing how, what, and why it had appeared. It was making its way towards the painting, and when it approached it, it collided with it, causing a rage of thunder and violent trembles. Moments later, the painting had completely vanished, replacing the old dust with new.

The town was suddenly screaming—it was as though it had been completely transformed. Zara rushed outside and found pandemonium in the streets. There were lots of people, cars, market stalls, and children running around, playing. Zara never told her father about the painting, and the town was completely oblivious to what had happened—it finally continued living on.

The next day, Zara decided to take a trip down to her basement. It was totally empty, except for one thing. In the far corner, she could see a strange figure. As she tentatively walked up to it, she realized that it was the skeletal bones of a human.

The Empress' Jade Necklace

It was a rather daunting place to be, and the atmosphere felt very tense. The firm, authoritative voice was quite frightening, but the gentlemen beside her showed no signs of fear or intimidation. They walked to and fro about the room comfortably. *Why shouldn't they?* After all, it was here that they spent most of their time.

A tall, slim gentleman, dressed in a grey suit, walked casually up to the stand where she was sitting nervously.

"Now Miss Kent, could you please tell the court, in your own words, the events leading up to your encounter, and what exactly happened once you reached your destination?"

Miss Kent spoke out in a timid voice, beginning her story:

"It all started when I received a letter from my uncle,

informing me of his dear friend, Lex Knight's death. In it there was an address and a small key, and I followed my uncle's instructions to go to this address and retrieve a wooden box. He said that I would know what to do from there on." A sense of excitement began to rise in the tone of her voice and it was becoming evident that as she continued with her tale, she began to feel more at ease with the situation. Seeing the sudden change in her tone convinced the man that there was no way he would be able to interrupt her now, so he stood back and let her tell her story to the entire court.

"The key did unlock the door, and a red lacquer wooden box was sitting there. Inside it, I found three documents, and I discovered a part of what appeared to be some notes, a map, and a diary entry. I became fascinated by what I had found.

"An archaeologist named Lex Knight had discovered where the Chinese Empress, Yang Chen's tomb was situated. It is believed that the Empress lived during the years of about 3000 BC. There was a legend that the finest jade necklace lay there. Lex also had a partner named Marcus Williams. Lex's research was incomplete, and since hardly anyone had even heard about this jade necklace ... I decided that I was going to complete his research and find this artefact. Being an archaeologist myself, I was extremely fascinated and completely willing and able to take on this mission.

"The following day, I gathered my belongings, Lex's documents, and took the first flight to China. When I reached China, I booked into a hotel and decided to take a second look at Lex's notes. As I began to read through them, towards the end of the passage of writing, I found that he had not completed the last sentence. There were smears of ink all over the bottom of the paper—it seemed as though he may have been disrupted while he was writing it. I became suspicious about what could have happened and I decided to search for any records of Lex Knight on the Internet."

At that moment, one of the lawyers came forward, holding a sheet of paper, and handed it to the large, round man sitting on a raised platform. The judge examined it for a few moments:

> *Lex Knight, Archaeologist (1960-1991)*
> *Investigation carried out by Los Angeles Police Department. Lex Knight was found murdered near Beijing in China, 4 March, 1991. Case was closed and incomplete.*

"That's fine, Miss Kent," he grunted. "Please continue."

"That night, I did not sleep. I set out at about 4:30 a.m. to catch a train to Beijing, and from there, my adventure began. I trekked through the forest for hours, and when nightfall came, I camped there for a short while to rest. In the morning I woke up and continued my journey.

"I suddenly came to a halt and looked up to find the great temple of Buddha. My eyes lit up with excitement, and impatiently, I pulled out some of Lex's notes from my bag, a section of it read:

"'... The burial ground is directly opposite the Buddha temple. The eyes of the statue point specifically to the tomb of the Empress Ying Chen ... the tomb will have been built with many traps in order to guard the Empress ...'

"I then stepped into the temple. There were beautiful

and ornate patterns on the ceiling and walls and it was amazing how everything had been preserved so well for so long. There were four grand pillars at either side with magnificent carvings on them. The pillars led straight to an opulent statue of Buddha. It was made of pure gold and around it, and there were flowers and other offerings. I examined the statue very closely and saw that the idol's eyes were looking out towards a cluster of trees, which was East from where I was standing, so I hurried out of the temple directly towards the trees.

"When I got there, I saw no indication of an opening or gate to any tomb. As I sat and stared out into the bushes, I saw something white sparkle due to the rays of the sun. As I walked up to it, I found a white slab of marble laying on the ground, which had been covered up by the green foliage. It took some effort to lift it up, as it was quite firmly pressed into the ground. After opening it, I jumped into the hole."

At this point, the other barrister interrupted and in a condescending manner asked, "And with no idea how deep it was, or what was down there, you just decided to jump in? Miss Kent, this all seems rather like a fairytale that you have invented ... you expect us to believe that y—"

"Objection! Mr. Bracklesbury is patronizing Miss Kent!" a voice spoke out in her defence.

"Mr. Bracklesbury, that will be quite enough! You have no right to patronize Miss Kent, now sit down!" Judge Williamson commanded. "Please continue, Miss Kent, and preferably get to the more relevant part of the story, please, otherwise we will be here all week listening to your adventures!" he stated.

"Yes, your honour ... em ... was dark and I ... oh yes ...

the walls were covered in Chinese writing, and pictures of presumably the Empress herself. It was like a narrow tunnel that at the end split into four. Each entrance had a Chinese symbol marked on it. They read north, south, east, and west. All of a sudden, one of my books dropped and fell in front of the north tunnel as I walked past it. At once, a large spear shot out from the left side of that tunnel and hit the other side. My heart pounded fearfully as I shifted myself towards the east tunnel. I carried on through the east tunnel, when suddenly my foot began to slide forward. I looked down and found that the ground began to shake and started crumbling fast; in a panic I grabbed the pillar at the side and pulled myself towards it.

"The tunnel became harder to follow, but eventually I reached the sarcophagus. I slid the white stone lid to open it and there lay the Empress, Ying Chen. She was dressed beautifully in elaborate red and gold organza silk, and around her neck glistened the jade necklace. There were also emeralds, amethysts, rubies, sapphires, and opals scattered all around her body. At her feet, there was a scroll with golden tassels on it. It contained information about the life of the Empress, from birth to death.

"Then I came back home and informed the LA Police Department and the museum about my discovery."

Mr. Bracklesbury spoke, "So you're saying that you just looked at the sarcophagus, came back to LA, and immediately informed the museum and the police?"

"Yes," she replied.

Mr. Bracklesbury continued, "Miss Kent, I'm not quite sure about a certain point you made earlier today. How did you come to know of Lex's death and get involved in this ... adventure?"

She sat calmly and replied, "I received a letter informing me about the death of Lex Knight."

"Ah, yes, and there was a key and address which you were told to go to? Is this the address?" He walked towards her holding a piece of paper with the address written on it, wanting her to confirm that it was correct. She nodded.

He then asked, "Do you know who killed Lex?" She was about to answer no to this rhetorical question when she was interrupted with the explanation.

"In Lex's notes, he mentioned camping near a tribal group the night he was killed. No weapons or evidence was found to point out who the murderer was, so the case was closed on the count of being incomplete. People then came to the conclusion that he was probably murdered by the tribal people. However, the case has now reopened due to the discovery of a vital piece of evidence." He swayed himself across the courtroom towards the judge, waving a polythene bag in his hand with a blood-stained knife inside it. They found this small knife buried beneath the soil with strange engravings on it. It was identified as a tribal knife, but the strange thing is, when we got a DNA sample taken from it, it matched Miss Kent's." The courtroom was suddenly completely silent for a few moments. The men and women sitting in the stands had stopped shuffling, the judge's chair stopped creaking, but after a moment the silence was interrupted by the heavy breathing and pounding heartbeat of Miss Kent.

"Miss Kent, where is that letter, key, and set of instructions that were given to you by your uncle?"

"I don't have it," Miss Kent said, uncomfortably.

"Why?" He was persistent.

"I lost it! But I ..."

Lucia

It was approaching the mid-twentieth century, and there were only two names at the top of the film industry, Daisy and her biggest rival, Lucia. The Chicago newspapers were at their peak, as juicy gossip was thrown out daily. Both young and beautiful they were, but one lacked the compassion and softness that the other had. Apart from that, they were both equally good actresses, which meant that neither could have the spotlight to themselves whilst the other was in the way. A wall of hatred built up between them, and each was constantly trying to win the crowd over. Daisy was quite an abrupt character, and had a tendency not to make full use of her common sense (as her advisors would say).

Lucia, on the other hand, had the expression of an innocent, sweet child, and was very soft spoken. Daisy often argued that this was all a scam, and another one of

Lucia's dirty acts. Lucia was married to a handsome barrister, and lived in the most luxurious palace in the whole of the city. It was in a concealed part of the city, where the family could maintain their privacy and escape the hounding paparazzi and newspapers. It was an incredibly quiet place, where the chaos of the city could not touch it. The house was a pure white colour, with cylindrical marble pillars before the ivory-bordered door. Inside, there was every comfort, even beyond imagination. In the hallway, the sparkling chandeliers hung proudly from the patterned ceiling, and the dining room walls were filled with the landscape paintings of Allston Washington.

In the summer, the lush, green garden was filled with the vibrant smell of jasmine, and the pink and purple blossoms on the trees glistened radiantly. Even in the winter when the snowfall came, it beautifully coated the surroundings like icing on a cake.

December 30, 1941. The malicious episode struck.

The headlines read:

"LUCIA HAS BEEN MURDERED!"

"OUR BELOVED LUCIA HAS BEEN TAKEN AWAY FROM US ... BUT WE WILL HAVE OUR JUSTICE ..."

The entire city grieved over the death of their beloved Lucia. Fans were depressed, angry and in want of justice. The investigation had begun and there were three people in question, because they were the ones who were found at the crime scene. This was a special case, and as the police department was very cautious as to finding the "fiend" who did this, the three suspects were kept hostage at the crime scene under strict surveillance.

The first to be questioned was of course Daisy, Lucia's well known rival.

"Now, Daisy, can you please tell us about what you were doing and where you were on the night of December 30th?"

She spoke in her sweet, Southern accent, "I certainly will, Lieutenant Briggs. Why, I was here at the Red House all night—it was poka' night. I was with John and Alyssa."

"Now I'm not an expert on card games, but for poker, don't you need to have four players?"

"Yes ... well later that night, Lucia waltzed right in here with a ... em—thinkin' she was all high and mighty as she usually does. Well Alyssa thought it would be a good idea to get Lucia to play, and well, John said it would make a great headline for the newspaper: 'Lucia goes bankrupt playin' poka!'" she giggled.

"Who are John and Alyssa?"

"John works for the Chicago press—he's my fiancé," she laughed, showing the lieutenant the big, shiny rock on her finger.

"... oh and Alyssa is just friend of mine."

"Okay, so what happened next? Did Lucia play?"

"Play what?"

"Poker, Miss Daisy ..."

"Yes, yes ... she sat down, thinkin' she was better than me ... an—"

"Miss Daisy, I—"

"Please ... call me Daisy, besides it won't be Miss for long, you know!"

"Yes, well, did you kill Lucia?"

"Wha—? No, of course I didn't. I can't believe you'd think that I would do such a thing. Is that why you're questioning me? Because if it is I refuse to answer any more of your dumb questions," she broke out into a strop and began to sob.

"No, Daisy, I'm just trying to get to the bottom of this. Please ... please could you tell me what else you know about that night?"

"Well ... I do know who *did* shoot Lucia. It was Tony, *her husband*. John and I were in the back talkin' to Randy, while Lucia was waitin' outside. Then, around eleven o'clock that night, we heard him storm in and yell, 'Lucia, what the heck are you doin' here?' He sounded so angry, and we didn't here anything from Lucia. Well we just stayed in the back, thinkin' that it was best that we stay out of husband and wife affairs ... well the next thing we heard was a gunshot. He must have been so furious that he shot her right there. As soon as we heard the shot, we ran out and we saw him there, in front of us, standin' over Lucia's dead body."

"Did anyone else see this apart from you, John, and Alyssa?"

"No, by that time the place had all cleared out, and Alyssa had left by about ten thirty, so she wadn't there either."

"Thank you, that'll be all the questions for now. You can go back up to your room."

"Lieutenant, how long am I gonna have to stay here? I missed my manicure appointment this morning cause of this!"

"Until we get to the bottom of this," he replied.

The next in line for questioning was Tony, but the only thing he had to say was that he did not shoot his wife. However, he also added the fact that he came into the Red House with Lucia, and that small slipup in Daisy's speech, which she thought the lieutenant took no notice of, confirmed that something was not right.

The lieutenant called for John, the reporter, next, and as suspected, there was no alteration and no difference to what Daisy had said. He too agreed that Tony shot Lucia.

These suspects had no idea what the police were up to, and while they thought that they were safe, both the pathologists and police uncovered something very interesting. The police found that John had been working on a new story for the newspaper, with the headline, "LOVING WIFE KILLED BY CRAZED HUSBAND."

The pathologists discovered that Lucia had not only been shot twice, but also she had been poisoned. Meanwhile, in Daisy's apartment, the police discovered an interesting, scrunched up letter in the trash can. It read:

> *... I know you're just using John so that you can boost your career ... I'm warning you, you better stay away from him or else I'm going to tell him about Cindy. You probably haven't mentioned the fact that you have a daughter, and you better think about the fact that when he finds out, he won't be happy. He's a good friend of mine and there's no way I'm going to let you use and ruin him. You have one week to break it off. You don't really love him, and what you're doing is wrong—you won't get away with it, so it would be in your best interests to tell him the truth and break it off ...*
>
> *Your well-wisher, Lucia*

The next day, Lieutenant Briggs approached John and Daisy with a few more questions.

"I wanted to let you know that we have just found some

interesting details of Lucia's death. You see, we could already see that she had been shot, but the medical tests that we have just got back indicate traces of poison in Lucia's blood."

"Really? Wow ... now that Tony really is somethin'! How did he do it?"

"Well, that's what I wanted to ask you both. I was wondering if you had any ideas about how and why he did this? I mean, the thing that puzzles me is that why would he go through so much trouble to kill his wife if he was planning on shooting her anyway?"

John suggested a theory, "Maybe he poisoned her first, but when he saw that the poison hadn't worked, he wanted to find her and finish it. Then that's when he came in here and shot her, I guess."

"Yes ..." The lieutenant began to think, "Thank you ... that was very helpful. Say, you ever thought about becoming a detective?" he laughed.

As soon as the letter had been found in Daisy's apartment, the police had begun their search for Cindy, but tracking her down was far too difficult. They were under a lot of pressure, as it had been almost three weeks, and yet there was no solid evidence to charge any one person with murder, as each had an air of guilt in their testimonies. However, the lieutenant was beginning to get a clearer picture of what may have happened that night, but again there was no proof to support his theory.

Into the late hours of the night, he sat in his office, going through all of the evidence and pondering over each person's account of the events that night. The office door opened and Chief Woodburrow walked in, taking a seat in front of Lieutenant Briggs.

"Briggs! We can't keep those three in that Red House forever. You and your team are going to have to do something, and fast. I'm under a lot of pressure from the mayor, who is getting more and more impatient every day. He's not happy about everything that's going on. I know you're doing your best and I've tried my best to hold off that pompous idiot for as long as I can, but … I'm giving you three more days. After three days, if one of them is not proven guilty of the crime, then they will be allowed to go free. We can't keep them locked up in there like prisoners without real evidence! We've already overstepped our boundaries." He had a deep, loud voice. He spoke in an authoritative, yet understanding tone.

"But, Chief, I know who did it! I just need more time to find the pr—"

"You have three days. Well, what was the motive?"

"The motive was this," he said, handing him the letter written by Lucia. Suddenly, Lieutenant Briggs stopped and seemed completely lost for a moment. Within five minutes he was out of sight, shouting "Chief—I've got it!"

The police provided backup for Lieutenant Briggs, and word had gotten out that the Red House was the place to be tonight because "somethin' big was goin' down." News reporters and photographers had all gathered around outside the Red House, impatiently waiting and anxious.

"Miss Daisy, you're under arrest for the murder of Lucia."

"What! This is ridiculous! You have no proof!"

"Actually, ma'am, we do. We found your daughter Cindy, and we asked her a few questions about her whereabouts on the night of the murder. Daisy, your daughter poisoned Lucia and—"

"Briggs! You leave her out of this!" she exclaimed.

"—and she did it because *you* told her to. However, the poor girl dropped half of it on the floor when pouring it into Lucia's drink. We found it, behind the bar," he said, holding up a small bag with some white powder in it.

He continued, "You knew that Lucia was going to expose the truth about you, and you couldn't risk losing it all could you? You would have lost everything if everyone found out that you had a child. So, when you realised that something had gone wrong with the poison, you shot her. Isn't that right, Miss Daisy?"

Daisy replied, scornfully, "She was pure evil. She couldn't stand the thought of me being happy—she wanted to ruin me. I had to do something ... I ..."

"Officers, did you get that?"

"Yes, Lieutenant," they answered.

Daisy was completely oblivious to the trick that the lieutenant had just played on her. "Lieutenant, what's goin' on?"

"Miss Daisy, you see, we did not have any solid evidence against you ... well ... I'm sorry we had to do it this way. Shall we go?"

Daisy had no choice but to follow, and as she was escorted out of the building, the paparazzi were out there waiting for her, and the next day her picture would be on the front cover of every local newspaper:

"DAISY IS NOT QUITE THE INNOCENT FLOWER THAT WE THINK SHE IS!"

Printed in the United Kingdom
by Lightning Source UK Ltd.
103145UKS00001B/400-447